To my daughters, Kelsey and Kylie
– Danette

The Proud Button written by Danette Richards and illustrated by Annelies Vandenbosch

ISBN 978-1-60537-607-3

This book was printed in April 2021 at Nikara, M. R. Štefánika 858/25, 963 01 Krupina, Slovakia.

First Edition
10 9 8 7 6 5 4 3 2 1

Clavis Publishing supports the First Amendment and celebrates the right to read.

WRITTEN BY DANETTE RICHARDS
ILLUSTRATED BY ANNELIES VANDENBOSCH

The PROUD Button

Clavis
NEW YORK

Meet Isabelle.
She's interested in lots of
things and she loves to play.

There was only one thing
missing: friends.
She just didn't think she could
make friends since she never
had a friend before.

Every time she tried to make a friend, her nerves seemed to get in the way.
Isabelle thought to herself, *I don't want the treasures*
in my treasure jar to be my only friends.
I want to make real friends too!

When Isabelle got home, her dad asked, "Isabelle, did you have fun?"

Isabelle responded, "Dad, I want to play with friends, not just my treasures."

Isabelle's dad nodded and said, "Yes, Isabelle, you will. Friends can be a lot like your treasures. I know you'll figure it out."

The next day walking to the bus stop, Isabelle
thought about what her dad had said to her.

She thought, *Hmm, friends are like my special treasures.
But right now, I feel too afraid to ask someone to
sit with me on the bus. What if they say no?*
She wondered why she felt this way.

A few days later, Isabelle arrived at school a little late.
Everyone was already working together.

"Isabelle, would you like to work with your tablemates
or would you like to work alone? I'm sure Lily and Damon
would love for you to join them," her teacher said.
Lily and Damon looked up at her with big smiles.
Isabelle timidly smiled back at them, but her fear of making
friends kept her from asking them if she could join their group.

Instead, she worked alone. As she shared her finished work
in front of the class, she thought to herself, *It really would
have been more fun working with Lily and Damon.*

That same day, Isabelle got off the bus and walked the rest of
the way home. She turned around a few times and saw
her schoolmates laughing and having fun.

She wondered why she wasn't laughing
and having fun with them.

When she got home, a package and note were waiting for her!

Hi honey,

I thought of you and how proud you are of your special treasures. I just got back from France, where we visited an abandoned button factory. They used to make porcelain buttons there a long time ago. The buttons that couldn't be sold were thrown in a field next to the factory. The field is long and very deep. I dug for buttons and found a very special button for you. I thought you would like to add this one to your special treasures!

Love,

Aunt Nancy

Isabelle wondered to herself how her Aunt Nancy knew
how proud she was of her special treasures. She ran to talk
to her mom and show off her special new treasure.

"Mom! Aunt Nancy said I'm *proud* of my treasures!
What does it mean to be proud?"

Isabelle's mom responded,

IT MEANS THAT YOUR TREASURES MAKE YOU FEEL HAPPY
AND FULL OF JOY, AND BECAUSE OF THAT, YOU MAKE SURE
THAT YOU TAKE GOOD CARE OF THEM.

Isabelle thought for a little while.
"Mom, I want to be happy with *myself*
and not just my special treasures. I want
my classmates to treat me with care,
and I want to treat them with care too.
This button will remind me that friends
are special treasures, just like Dad said.

I'll call it my proud button.
That means I'll feel proud when I wear it,
proud of myself and proud of how I act every day."

treasure

Isabelle

Later that day, Isabelle's mom said,
"I sewed your proud button onto
your favorite coat. It's getting colder
and I thought you would like that."

That evening, Isabelle went to the clothing store
wearing her coat. Suddenly, she saw Damon, and she froze.
Just then, she remembered she had her proud button.
She touched the proud button on her coat and was reminded to
always be proud of herself and have confidence. With that thought,
she threw her hand high in the air, smiled, and waved. "Hi Damon!"
To her surprise, Damon waved right back and said,
"Hi Isabelle. What are you doing here?"

Isabelle felt like she just made a friend and was proud that
she had the courage she never knew she had before.

The next morning, Isabelle made sure that she wore
her proud button when she was walking to the school bus stop.
She saw Lily, who was already there waiting.
"Lily, would you like to sit with me on the bus today?" Isabelle asked.
She was scared to hear the answer, but she had to ask the question.
"Oh yes, that would be fun!" Lily said. "What's with the button?"

Isabelle told her it was a special treasure from her
Aunt Nancy and that she called it her proud button.

Feeling joyful and full of confidence after such a fun day, Isabelle went to the playground after school.

She walked right up to her other classmates,
Zoe and Sam, and said, "Can I play with you too?"
"Sure, you'll like this game!" they said.
Isabelle no longer felt timid and shy as she once did.
She now felt *proud* of herself.

What's happening? Isabelle thought in her bed at night.
I had the best day EVER! I think my proud button really works!
I'm proud of myself. Now I know I can make friends. We make
each other happy and that's why we take good care of each other.

Friends are just like my special treasures, but even better!